Bob the Builder

Mucky Muck

After a rainy day the yard was full of
puddles. Dizzy was fed up.
"Please can we go out and play?"
she asked Bob.

"No, Dizzy," he said. "You'll get dirty, just like
Scoop and Muck."

"But it's lovely being dirty!" cried Muck.

Wendy was at the farm, repairing the guttering on Farmer Pickles's roof.

"How's it going?" Farmer Pickles shouted up to her.

"It doesn't look good," Wendy replied.

"You haven't just got a broken gutter, there's a crack in the drainpipe too. Lofty and I have got quite a bit of work to do."

Back at the yard, Bob put on his apron and filled up a
bucket with warm, soapy water.

"Who's first for a wash?" he asked.

"Ooh, me please!" giggled Dizzy.

"You're not even dirty!" laughed
Bob. "I'll start with Scoop."

Muck huddled up close to Roley.

"I'm glad I'm not first. I don't want
to be washed. I love being mucky."

"That's why you're called Muck!"
chuckled Roley.

Bob covered Scoop in soapy bubbles, then connected the hose pipe to the tap, so that he could rinse him clean. He didn't realise that his foot was on the hose pipe, blocking off the water.

"What's going on?" wondered Bob as he peered down the empty nozzle. Suddenly he lifted up his foot and the water swooshed out, all over his face and all over the yard.

"Oohh, noooo!" spluttered Bob.

Meanwhile, Spud had been sheltering from the rain in Travis's trailer.

When he saw it had stopped, he threw back the waterproof cover he'd been lying under and jumped out.

"Thanks, Travis," he said. "I hate getting wet."

"That's all right," said Travis and revved up his engine to move forward. His wheels span around, but Travis didn't move. He was stuck tight in the deep mud.

"I'll never get out!" he wailed.

"Hang on," said Spud. "I'll go and get Farmer Pickles."

Back at the yard, Bob had just finished giving Scoop a wash down. His yellow paintwork gleamed brightly. "Right, now it's your turn, Muck," said Bob.

"Can Roley go before me?" he begged.

"You're not frightened of a drop of water, are you?" laughed Bob.

"No, of course not," said Muck, very nervously.

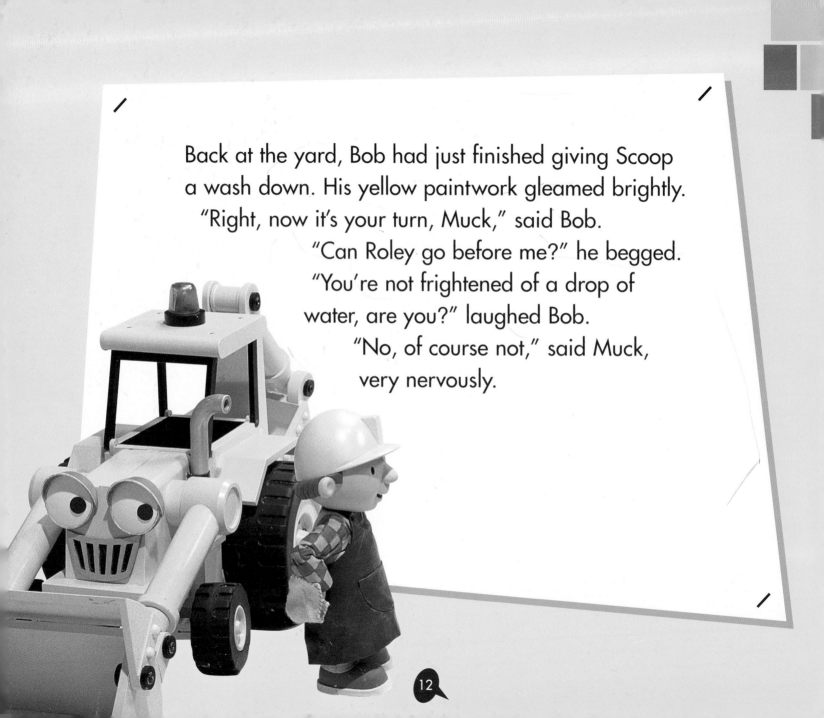

12

Just then, Bob's mobile phone started ringing.

"Hang on, Muck," he said. When he'd finished his call, Bob turned to the machines, "That was Farmer Pickles. Travis is stuck in the mud," he said.

"I can pull him out!" cried Scoop.

"Your wheels might get stuck too," said Bob. "I think I'll use Muck. His caterpillar treads are built for this kind of job."

"That's lucky," Muck whispered to Roley. "Now I can stay mucky!"

"Bob, please can I come too?" asked Dizzy.

"All right," said Bob.

"Hurray!" squeaked Dizzy.

"**Can we help him?**" Bob called out.

"**Yes, we can!**" the machines shouted back.

Bob, Muck and Dizzy set off for the farm.
"Emergency! Woo! Woo!" squeaked Dizzy, pretending
to have a siren like a police car.

When they arrived at the field, they
could see that Travis was well and
truly stuck.

"Don't worry, Travis," called Bob.
"We'll have you
out in no time."

16

Bob tied one end of a rope around Travis's axle and the other end to Muck's tow bar.

"Can you tow it, Muck?" he called.

"**YES**... hummpf!" spluttered Muck as he struggled to turn his big caterpillar wheels. "**I**... Ufff! **CAN!**" said Muck tugging hard.

Suddenly Travis's wheels started to spin and then they both shot forwards, sending a shower of mud everywhere!

When Travis was free from the mud, Farmer Pickles thanked Bob. "Do you fancy a nice glass of apple juice after all that hard work?" he asked.

"Good idea," Bob replied. They both climbed into Travis's trailer. Then Travis led the way to the farmhouse, followed by Muck and Dizzy.

As they trundled along the lane Spud popped up, holding a big, sloppy mud pie.

"Hey, Dizzy, over here!" he called. Dizzy turned around and Spud threw the mud pie straight into her face. Splat! Mud trickled down Dizzy's nose making her giggle.

"Oooh, it's all squishy!" she squealed. Spud threw an even bigger mud pie at Muck.

"A mud pie fight!" yelled Muck. In their excitement, Dizzy and Muck forgot all about keeping up with Travis and Bob.

When Bob arrived at the farmhouse he found Lofty and Wendy fitting the last section of guttering.

"How are you getting on?" he called up to her.

"Fine," Wendy replied. "So you managed to pull Travis out of the mud?"

"Yes. Muck did well, didn't you?" Bob said as he turned around to talk to Muck. But the digger machine wasn't there. "Where have Muck and Dizzy gone?" he gasped.

Muck was still having a wonderful time in the field.

"If I was as little as you, Dizzy, I'd roll over and wriggle in this lovely, squishy mud!" he said.

"**Wheee!**" squeaked Dizzy as she flipped onto her back and rolled in the mud like a little puppy.

Suddenly they heard Bob's voice. "Dizzy! Muck! What's going on?" he shouted.

"Er, we were just having a game of mud pies," muttered Muck.

"We were worried. You had all better get back to the farm, right now," said Bob. "Farmer Pickles has got a surprise for you."

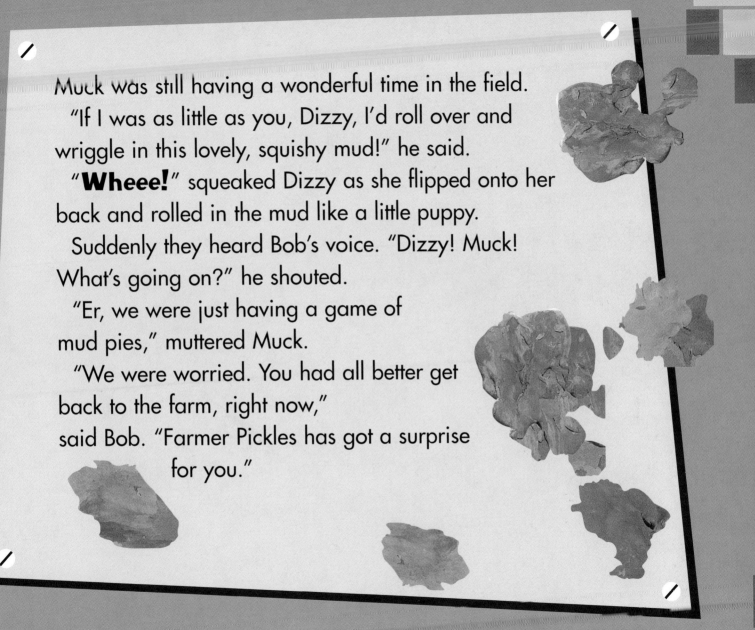

Back at the farm, Bob lined up Muck, Dizzy and Spud, and told them to close their eyes.

"Ooh, I hope it's something really scrummy!" said Spud hungrily.

"Ready?" Bob asked, as Wendy and Farmer Pickles came out of the house with buckets of soapy water.

"Ready!" laughed Wendy.

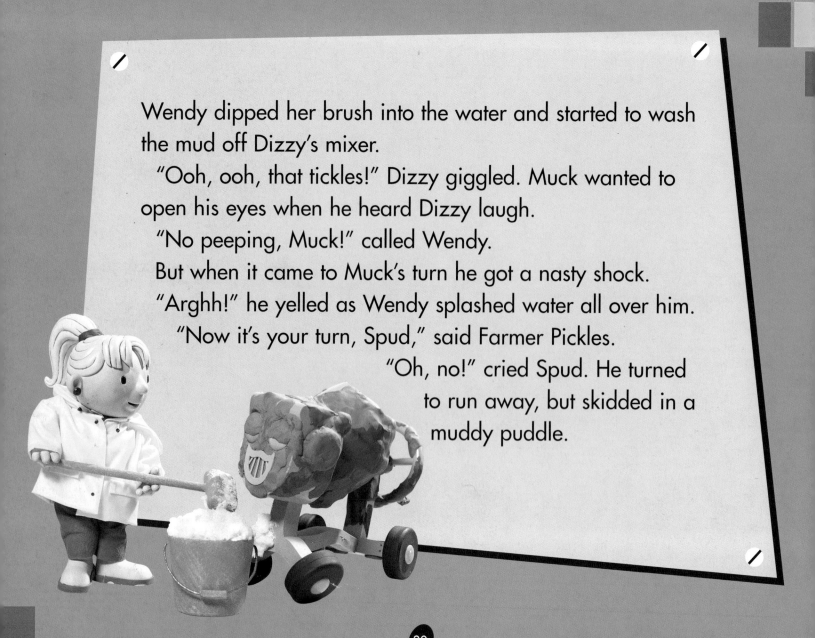

Wendy dipped her brush into the water and started to wash the mud off Dizzy's mixer.

"Ooh, ooh, that tickles!" Dizzy giggled. Muck wanted to open his eyes when he heard Dizzy laugh.

"No peeping, Muck!" called Wendy.

But when it came to Muck's turn he got a nasty shock.

"Arghh!" he yelled as Wendy splashed water all over him.

"Now it's your turn, Spud," said Farmer Pickles.

"Oh, no!" cried Spud. He turned to run away, but skidded in a muddy puddle.

"Owww!" Spud cried, as he fell flat on his face and bent his nose.

"Has anyone got a new parsnip?"

THE END!